WITH

Anne Rooney does not eat meat, in case the taste of blood becomes too appealing.

When not writing books she haunts the cemeteries and catacombs of Paris and Venice and raises non-vampiric daughters and chickens in Cambridge. She studied at a haunted college and her first car was a haunted van; the undead hold no fears for her.

With thanks to Hannah Frew, Mary Hoffman,
Shahrukh Husain and Professor Sunetra Gupta,
University of Oxford.

Every Drop of your Blood

by Anne Rooney
www.annerooney.co.uk

Published by Ransom Publishing Ltd.
Radley House, 8 St. Cross Road, Winchester, Hants.
SO23 9HX, UK
www.ransom.co.uk

ISBN   978 184167 299 1

First published in 2012
Reprinted 2013

A CIP catalogue record of this book is available from the British Library.

Vampire
Dawn

Every Drop
of your
Blood

ANNE ROONEY

Ransom

Hungary, August ...

Juliette, Omar, Finn, Ruby and Alistair find a dead body in the forest ...

... Twenty-four hours later, they tie the murderer, Ava, to a tree, as one by one they fall sick ...

... When they wake, they are vampires, and that murderer looks rather appealing ...

... Mysterious nobleman Ignace, 400 years old and more sophisticated than is good for him, prevents them snacking on her ...

... But that dead body isn't as dead as it looked ...

... They go to Ignace's castle for a crash-course in being a modern vampire.

And so their adventures begin.

This is Omar's story ...

One

'Passport?'

The guard didn't look up until Omar handed his passport over. Then he did.

'Iraqi? What will you be doing in the United States?' the guard asked.

'Work experience,' Omar answered, and smiled. He was looking forward to working in a research laboratory for a few weeks. The man didn't smile back.

'This is a tourist visa – you can't work on it. You're an Iraqi trying to enter the United States on the wrong visa. Get over there.'

And so the nightmare began.

Two armed guards hustled Omar into a hot room crowded with frightened people. There weren't enough seats, and no food or drink. He'd spent eight impatient hours on a jumbo jet to New York. Now all his excitement turned to fear.

Soon he was dragged out and pushed into an interview room. They gave him a glass of water and fired questions at him until his head was reeling.

'I'm sorry, I'm confused,' he said. 'I've had a long flight, I'm tired. I don't understand ... '

A man with a gun slammed his hand on the

table in front of Omar.

'Just answer the questions. Who sent you to the United States?'

'No one. I'm here for work experience, I told you,' Omar said. It was getting scary. He was in a padded room with three large men carrying guns – and they weren't on his side.

'Who are you working for? What will you be doing?' the man asked, leaning close to Omar's face.

'It's a laboratory, the Gamaleya Institute. It's doing virus research. I'm going to university to do biology and ... ' Omar was starting to panic.

The man interrupted him.

'Who runs this laboratory? Who organised this 'work experience'?'

Omar stalled. He could hardly say 'a vampire I met in Hungary organised it'.

'Answer!' the man shouted.

'A man called Ignace,' Omar said. 'I ... I met him in Europe. I don't know his second name.'

The man typed on a keyboard, waited a moment, then looked hard at him.

'This Institute doesn't exist. So,' he said with a sneer, 'you are Iraqi – '

'I'm a British citizen!' Omar interrupted. 'I'm allowed to live in Britain!'

'You are Iraqi,' the man continued, 'you're trying to enter the US on a tourist visa but you intend to work – illegally – on viruses in a research estab-lishment which doesn't exist. This isn't looking good, is it? Do you have links with any terrorist organisations? Are you working on germ warfare?'

'NO!' Omar shouted, and two hands clamped his shoulders immediately. Instinctively, he twisted away from the hands, and then everything went black.

* * * * *

When he opened his eyes, Omar was in a white room. It was empty except for the bed he lay on. Bars of shadow on the floor led his eye to a heavy, steel door with a barred window. Not a room, then – a cell.

He put a hand to his head, which ached, then raised himself on one elbow. He felt sick. What had happened? Where was he?

Slowly, it came back to him. The interview room, shouting. Words floated into his mind: 'terrorist', 'Iraqi scum', 'Egypt', 'make you tell us'.

Tell them what? Tell who what? Someone had handcuffed him and dragged him somewhere. He lay back on the bed and tried to remember.

He'd drunk some water, but it had tasted funny. Was that because it was American water, or was it drugged? Omar reached for his phone – but his pocket was gone. He looked down: he was in a green jumpsuit. He had no memory of getting changed, or of anyone removing his clothes. He did a mental tour of his body and couldn't feel anything hurting apart from his head, so they hadn't hit him or anything. Yet.

Suddenly, there was a clang and the scrape of

metal against stone, then the door opened. Omar sat up, expecting to see an armed guard. Instead he saw a stooped old man with brown skin, thin arms and legs, and strings of long black hair. He carried a covered plate and wore a tunic something like a Roman toga. Where he should have had eyes, a broad band of scar tissue spread from one side of his face to the other.

The man walked straight to the side of the bed without stumbling and put the plate on the floor.

'Is that what will happen to me?' Omar blurted out.

The man opened his mouth and pointed to the stub of tongue that was all he had left. Then he went, closing the door behind him.

Two

The sight of the broken old man frightened Omar as much as the guards had done – perhaps more.

He lifted the cover from the plate, wondering what they were giving him. A chunk of raw meat. And a ProVamp capsule – the supplements that vampires took in place of human blood. So they knew he was a vampire. He heard a laugh outside, and the door opened again.

'How are you, Omar?' The tall, familiar figure of Ignace filled the doorway. Relief and anger swirled around in Omar's mind.

'Is this your idea of a joke?' he shouted.

'I'm sorry,' Ignace said, 'it was tricky to get you here any other way. Our people in security in New York are a bit – keen. You're not hurt, I hope?'

'Where is 'here'?'

'Russia. Near Yakutsk. Well, near-ish. We're just south of the Arctic circle, in the forest. But don't worry – it's warm inside.'

'I'm not worried about the weather. I want to know what I'm doing here.'

Ignace put his fingertips together, making a triangle of space between his hands.

'You *would* be worried about the weather if you tried to go outside. You're doing what you agreed to do: work experience. But at a rather higher level than you were expecting, I think.'

'I'm supposed to be in New York, not Russia! How did I get here? What's going on?'

Ignace was calm.

'My people in the airport were waiting for you. They drugged you and put you on a plane here. They told you – and homeland security – they were sending you to the Middle East for a little softening up. Now – '

'You can't just abduct people!' Omar cried. 'You kidnapped me! That's ... I mean, you can't – '

Ignace ignored him.

'You wanted to work in a laboratory before starting your course in biology, is that right?'

'Aren't you going to answer me?' Omar was furious.

'No,' said Ignace. 'You're going to answer *me*. You wanted to work in a laboratory?'

Omar realised he wasn't going to get anywhere complaining. 'Yes. This is a funny place for an interview,' he said.

'Quite. But you aren't going anywhere else just yet. And you're going to Oxford University next year?'

'Yes.'

'Clever lad. Just what I need. Eat your lunch and we'll get started.'

Ignace went out, leaving the door open. Omar swallowed the ProVamp capsule and walked to the door. A long corridor stretched ahead of him, lined with steel doors the same as his. They were all closed.

To the right, the corridor turned a corner. To the left, an iron grille cut off the last few feet. Behind it stood a heavy wooden door. Thick bars crossed the door frame, secured to the rough stone with huge bolts.

Omar went to look. A chain as thick as his arm wound over the bars, and a yellowing notice hung from a nail on the door. It showed a picture of a black eagle, wings spread wide, and beneath it in red:

'Eintritt verboten.' Entry forbidden. In German.

'Hello?' Omar called softly. He heard shuffling and the sudden clank of a chain behind the door, and then footsteps behind him. Ignace was walking quickly along the corridor.

'Good – you've finished. This way, please.'

Omar stood looking at the door the other side of the metal grille.

'What's in there?' he asked.

'Nothing to concern you. We're going this way.' Ignace took his arm, firmly.

'My door was open,' Omar said.

'Of course – you're not in prison! You're simply working for me for a while. As you agreed.'

'And then I can go home?'

'Naturally. If your work goes well.'

'And if not?' Omar asked, almost running to keep up with Ignace.

'Here we are.'

The room they entered was completely white, with a vaulted ceiling. Laboratory benches ran in rows all through it, and people in lab coats bustled around. There was equipment Omar had seen only in TV documentaries.

'This is your bench,' Ignace said. 'You can have anything you need – there's no limit.'

At one end of the bench stood a stylish computer and a stack of papers.

'What do I have to do?' Omar asked.

'I told you we think vampirism is caused by a virus,' Ignace explained. 'Well, we need to be sure. That's where you come in.

'Most of the work has been done by Mr Pasteur. You've heard of him, I expect – a very distinguished scientist. He discovered bacteria, and produced a vaccine against a virus.'

'In the 1880s?' Omar asked.

An older man in a lab coat appeared beside Ignace.

'Starting in the 1870s, actually. Rabies, it was.' The man spoke with a French accent. 'Pleased to meet you, young man. Louis Pasteur.' He dipped his head slightly, revealing a bald patch, and held out a hand to Omar. 'Welcome.'

Omar was stunned. 'You're Louis Pasteur? But – you died in 1895!'

'Don't believe everything you read on Wikipedia, young man.' Pasteur chuckled. 'I had a very grand funeral – *and* I got to go to it! They buried someone else, you know. Don't worry, he was dead. And I got a new job – here! Best lab in the world!

'The hard work,' Pasteur went on, 'is done by that man over there.' He pointed to a tall, thin figure at the far side of the room who looked more like a ghost than anyone Omar had ever seen. His skin was as pale as porcelain, and his beard and remaining hair were snow-white. The man waved a gloved hand holding a scalpel.

'Dmitri Ivanovski,' Pasteur shouted across the

room. 'Come and meet our new scientist.' The man carefully laid down his scalpel and paced between the benches.

Pasteur slapped him on the back and Ivanovski flinched. He bowed to Omar. 'Delighted,' he said.

'Dmitri here,' Pasteur went on, 'discovered viruses. Good work, eh?' Ivanovski smiled briefly. Omar looked from one to the other, stunned.

'Now, let me show you my work.'

Pasteur took Omar's arm and led him through the lines of benches to one covered with dishes, microscope slides and bottles of chemicals. A dead dog lay in a large tray.

'What I did before was, I took the spinal cords from rabbits with rabies and I gave them to dogs, and the dogs did not get rabies. Good, eh? And then I gave them to people, and people did not get rabies. But I cannot take the spinal cords from vampires, eh?' He chortled and his shoulders shook.

'But you did, Louis,' Ivanovski called from his own bench.

'Ah yes. It didn't work. It didn't work.'

'What didn't work?' asked Omar.

'A vampire ... had an accident. It happens. I took the spinal cord, I dried it, powdered it, I fed it to a person – and he became a vampire! It is awful! It was supposed to protect him.'

Omar opened his mouth to speak. But before he could say anything, Ignace put a hand on his shoulder.

'Come. You start work tomorrow. Now I'll show you where you'll sleep.'

'Not in that room?'

Ignace laughed.

'Good grief, no. That's a holding cell. You're our guest.'

'Cell? You have prisoners?' asked Omar.

Ignace didn't reply. He just led him out of the lab.

Three

Omar's room was large, luxurious and warm. The window looked out onto a floodlit forest thick with snow. More snow fell from the dark sky, swirling in the lights. In front of the trees, he could just make out lines of razor wire. It was hard to see, steel against snow.

'There's a map of the castle on the desk. You may go anywhere that's not locked,' Ignace said. 'Your luggage has been put away. I'm sorry about the jumpsuit. We had to pretend, you see, that you were our prisoner. Now please rest. I'll see you tomorrow.'

Omar didn't mean to sleep. He lay on the bed and watched the snowflakes. But in a few moments, he fell into a deep sleep.

When he woke, pale sunlight filled the room. He showered and dressed. As soon as he tied his trainers, there was a knock at the door and Ignace came in. It made Omar feel uncomfortable: had Ignace been watching or listening?

'Good morning,' Ignace said. 'I hope you slept well?' He didn't wait for an answer. 'Come – I want you to meet my subjects.'

'Your subjects? Are you a king?'

'No. You misunderstand. The subjects of my experiments. This way.'

Ignace led him through a maze of corridors and winding staircases. This part of the castle was not like the lab. It was more like a castle should be – old, crumbling stone with battered doors that creaked and groaned on their hinges.

At last, they stepped outdoors into a courtyard and the cold slammed into Omar. He trod in Ignace's footsteps through the deep snow. Then Ignace punched a long code into a keypad beside an iron door. Omar watched, memorising the numbers: 2, 0, 0, 4, 1, 8, 8, 9.

This part of the castle was even older – and colder. The walls sparkled with frost and thin arrow-slits let in only a little light. They went through a rusting gate.

It was a gateway into hell.

Omar reeled in horror, stepping backwards against the stone wall. He wanted to run, but where to? Iron cages lined the room. Each cage held a single human being, thin, ragged and desperate. There were twenty or thirty altogether.

When they saw Ignace, the people cowered at the backs of their cages. Some covered their faces. They were trying to hide, Omar realised. To hide, in a bare cage. 'Don't choose me,' they were saying silently.

'What is all this?' Omar gasped. 'Who are they?'

'Why, my subjects!' Ignace smiled. 'Don't worry, they don't stay here for long. They're held here for detox.'

'Where do they come from?' Omar whispered, unable to take it in.

'The markets.'

'Markets? You can't buy people in markets!'

'Of course you can,' said Ignace. 'If you know where to look. You think humans are so great, don't you? We're not the barbarous ones. If *they* didn't sell them, I couldn't buy them. Which would you like?'

'What?'

'Choose – you'll need one for practice.'

'I – I don't want one!' Omar cried. 'I won't have anything to do with this, whatever it is!'

'No matter. I'll choose, then. I expected scientific curiosity. How disappointing.'

'You can't experiment on these people. It's cruel! It's appalling!' Omar said.

Ignace laughed.

'What do you think would happen to them otherwise? In the flesh markets? Come: let's go to the laboratory and you can start work.'

Ignace led the way back and Omar had no option but to follow him, but this time as he crossed the courtyard he scanned it for an escape route. The walls towered above him, dark and shiny with ice.

* * * * *

Back in the laboratory, Ignace behaved as

though nothing had happened.

'As you can see, we have some great people here,' he said. 'But sometimes it's difficult to think in new ways. That's why you're here. A fresh approach.'

Omar felt sick. But he had to stay calm, have time to think. He flicked through the papers piled on his bench.

'What do you want me to do?' he asked.

'Look at the figures. Work out why this 'virus' isn't acting like a virus. We need to know how it spreads.'

'But don't you know already?' Omar was confused.

'Not exactly. It didn't matter so much before,' Ignace said. 'Once we developed ProVamp, it wasn't

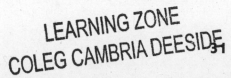
31

spreading. But now, with the mosquitoes ... We can't have them turning the whole world into vampires.'

Ignace left him, and Omar began reading. Pasteur and Ivanovski had heated vampire blood and injected it into the 'subjects', who often became vampires. The papers made Omar feel even more sick.

'So you see,' said Pasteur, appearing beside him, 'it's not caused by bacteria – they're destroyed by heat. But it's too robust for a virus. Even if we dry vampire blood for a week, it still carries the infection.'

'How about a parasite, like malaria?' Omar asked.

'Good idea, but no. We've examined the

mosquito from Hungary that bit you, and there are no parasites in it. Oh – and that mosquito? We sequenced the DNA. It's a type we've never seen before; we've called it *Culiseta coburnensi*. Maybe it's a mutation.'

'Why do you need me? I'm only a student,' Omar asked. 'Get someone better. I'd rather go home and do normal work experience.'

Pasteur rubbed his hands together.

'Ah, young man – you grew up with all this new science, but we struggle to keep up sometimes!' He laughed. 'I've been here a hundred years! I love it, but I'm a little stale. You're new blood – so to speak.'

four

Several days passed, with Omar reading papers and talking to Pasteur. He quickly grew to like him. Pasteur's enthusiasm was infectious. Omar wanted to solve the puzzle, to please Pasteur. But the memory of the cages haunted him.

One morning, Omar woke feeling jittery. Something was different. A hot shower didn't help. Was he ill? In the mirror, the brown of his skin was paler. He looked almost grey, like in a black and white photograph. He swallowed a ProVamp capsule from the bowl by the bed. Even that didn't make him feel better.

In the lab, Omar flicked a journal open and tried to read, but the words swam before his eyes.

'Louis, I don't feel well,' he said.

'Good.' Ignace had appeared silently by his desk. 'You're here. Come with me.' He either had not heard or did not care how Omar felt.

They went to the courtyard they'd crossed before. Omar shivered outside in his thin lab coat – not just with cold.

Back in the room of cages, he tried to keep his eyes on the ground. He felt a little better in here. The air smelled – alive, somehow. He looked up.

Some of the cages were empty. The remaining people were cowering again, but it alarmed him less. In fact, it annoyed him. What good was cowering going to do?

A girl in one cage stared back at him, dark eyes gleaming. Black hair fell over her shoulders and she flicked it back, defiant. Something in him responded. Ignace watched Omar silently and smiled.

'That one? Shall we take a look?' he said.

They walked over to the cage. Omar wondered why the girl wasn't trying to hide, like the others. She held his gaze, and he felt some need stir in him. Ignace beckoned the girl to the bars and she came closer, so close Omar could smell her.

Ignace unpinned an ornate brooch from his jacket, grabbed the girl's hand and pricked her finger ever so slightly with the pin. She tried to snatch her hand back, but Ignace held her wrist.

The girl shouted in a language Omar didn't understand, but the words curdled on the air as something else took over his mind. Blind hunger.

He saw the tiny spot of blood and wanted it, wanted her, more desperately than he had wanted anything since ... he couldn't remember. Yes, he could. Since he'd wanted Ava in the forest the day they had become vampires. He'd been ashamed of that afterwards, how he'd behaved. But now it was back, just as potent and alien and urgent. And he was shameless.

He grabbed the girl's hand, wiped the spot of blood onto his finger and licked it. He'd never tasted anything so wonderful. At that moment

Ignace released the girl's wrist. She fled to the back of the cage and pressed herself against the wall – just like all the others. Omar shook the bars and the girl hid her face in her hands.

'Later, perhaps,' Ignace said, putting a hand on his shoulder. 'We have other business today.'

To Omar it seemed as though he were on the edge of a diving board, longing to dive off but forced to go back. His body was electric and tight. He shuddered.

'Come on.' Ignace paced ahead. Omar didn't dare look back at the girl in the cage. 'Later' rang in his head, keeping his body tight and eager. Dragging himself away, he felt as though he were joined to the girl with elastic, the effort needed to pull away from her increasing with every step.

five

Ignace led him along a corridor to a warm room with a roaring fire, deep chairs, rugs and tapestries.

'Relax,' he said. 'There's someone I'd like you to spend a little time with. Alone.'

He opened a low door. A girl walked in, her head bowed. Blonde hair fell onto her shoulders. Ignace took her hand, and there was that brooch again. Omar wondered if Ignace ever sterilised it.

The pin prick was so slight it took several seconds for even a drop of blood to come. The girl didn't flinch. *Was she used to it?* Omar wondered. Ignace held the finger towards Omar for him to see and then slipped out of the door, closing it behind him. Omar was sure he would be watching and listening.

Omar looked back at the girl. The tiny smudge of blood didn't grow any bigger. He was curious, but that was all. He was more curious about her. There was something familiar about her. The tanned skin, blonde hair hanging loose, thin limbs. Then she lifted her head.

'Ava!'

'Omar?' She took a step back.

Of course. Last time they'd met, he'd tried to

attack her. She'd been tied to a tree. Ava had killed her boyfriend – or rather, she hadn't. She'd tried to nail him to the ground with a tent peg but had got it wrong. And he – Omar – had tied her to a tree and tried to bite her. He felt embarrassed. It wasn't a good start.

He talked, gibbered really, for a few minutes while she just looked at him. And then she said, 'It's good to see you. A familiar face. I don't like it here.'

'How did you get here?' he asked.

'I don't know. I just woke up here yesterday.'

'Where? In a – ' he didn't want to say 'cage'. He just stopped.

'In here. And I have another room, through

there. It's nice, but – I'm scared. Ignace said I had to stay a few days.'

So she wasn't one of Ignace's 'subjects'. Omar was relieved.

'I'm sorry,' he said. 'About – before.'

Ava shrugged. 'Everything's pretty weird.'

Minutes passed. When Ignace returned, he took Ava's hand and turned it towards Omar, showing him the red spot on her finger.

'Well?' Ignace asked. 'Aren't you interested? What's wrong?'

Omar realised he wasn't. When the woman in the cage bled, he was out of his mind with desire for her. When Ava bled, he just looked at it. Nothing stirred in him. Nothing at all. Yet when she had been tied to the tree ... What had happened?

'Lick it,' Ignace said.

'What?'

'Lick her finger.'

Omar didn't want to – it didn't feel right. But Ava held her hand out to him. He put his lips around her finger, and sucked gently like a kiss. It felt intimate and close, and odd to be doing it in this strange castle in front of Ignace. But it was a small thing, and soon over.

The warmth he felt was for the sun-bleached hairs curling over her tawny arm, the tan fading now. He looked at her wrist, so thin he could easily circle it with his fingers – and he wanted to circle it. But the blood did nothing to him.

'Nothing,' Ignace said decisively. Omar couldn't tell whether he was pleased or annoyed.

'Let's go.'

As Ignace hurried him out, Omar looked over his shoulder at Ava and mouthed to her: 'I'll get you out, if I can.'

Then the door closed and the sweet, sweet smell of the blood of the woman in the cage hit Omar like a punch. He staggered behind Ignace.

Six

Omar's muscles wanted the stretch of movement, and he wondered if that was why he felt so sick and weak. At home, he would be cycling, playing basketball or running. Activity helped him think, and he needed to think.

His research was going nowhere and he could see Pasteur beginning to doubt that he would come up with anything. Omar wanted to impress him. But he also feared he'd never get out unless he succeeded – or escaped.

Omar paced the corridors and twisting stairways of the castle. Once or twice he heard footsteps, but he didn't see anyone else. He walked on and on, thinking. He was certain now that they were not looking at a virus. But what was left?

He found himself in the corridor he'd been on the first day and walked up to the iron grille. *Eintritt Verboten*. Why in German? He tried to remember the code Ignace had used to get to the caged people. On the keypad, he pressed '2', then '0' then '0' again; '4', '1', '8', '9'.

An alarm wailed. Omar ran back down the corridor, round the corner – straight into Ignace, flanked by four men in riot gear carrying machine guns. Ignace grabbed both his shoulders.

'What do you think you're doing?' he shouted.

'I ... Nothing. I was just curious.'

'I told you – you can go anywhere that isn't locked. You deliberately disobeyed me. Why?'

Omar couldn't think of any reason.

'I meant no harm.'

'This isn't a game, Omar.' Ignace dismissed the armed guards. His voice was calmer, but still stern. 'Do you know the story of Bluebeard's castle?'

'Yeah, it's a kid's story. Girl marries a psycho and he gives her a bunch of keys to his castle, tells her not to open one door. She opens it. There are all his previous wives, hanging like Christmas-tree ornaments. Girl freaks out.'

'That's the one. I don't have a bunch of keys to give you. But there are doors that are open and doors that are not. That one is not. As you can see.'

'What's in there? Women strung up on meat hooks?' Omar wasn't sure whether it was a joke, even as he asked. After all, Ignace had shown him the room of cages – how bad did things have to be here to be hidden?

'I have things you don't need to see. Let's leave it at that. You'll never approach this gate again. Is that understood?'

Omar nodded. Ignace walked quickly away, his heels clicking on the stone floor. After a few metres, he stopped and turned back.

'And it's not a 'what', it's a 'who'. Hope that you never find out who's behind that door.'

Seven

Omar sat up with a start. It was the middle of the night, but his mind was buzzing. The gate hadn't opened because he'd got the numbers in the wrong order. Same numbers, wrong order. That was what they should be looking for – something to do with order. There was no bacterium, no virus, no parasite – it was the body going wrong from within.

He couldn't wait until dawn, so he dressed

quickly and hurried to the lab. Pasteur was at his bench, and smiled as he came in.

'Well, well. You've realised you don't need to sleep? It usually takes thirty years for that to kick in. So – what are you doing here?'

'I know what we're looking for, I think,' Omar said.

'Excellent! Don't tell me yet. Check first. I like to get all my excitement in one go. There's not much of it around these days.'

Pasteur chuckled, and went back to prodding a dead dog.

'What are you doing with that?' Omar asked.

'Nothing really – messing about. I can't make a vampire dog, whatever I do. I've bitten them, I've transfused blood into them, I've used vampire nervous tissue, saliva, everything. I don't have any more ideas. Don't tell Ignace.' He chuckled. 'He'll put me on one of his screwball projects if he thinks I'm not busy.'

'Have you tried other animals?' Omar asked.

'Rabbits – nothing. Horses – nothing. Just as well. Vampire horses would be a problem.'

'Bats?'

Pasteur laughed and shook his head.

Omar read everything he could find on prions – proteins that have gone wrong. Dogs, rabbits and horses don't get prion diseases. Most prion diseases take years to show up, crawling through the nervous system. But if vampirism were carried in the blood it could take effect very quickly. A blood cell goes all round the body in one minute.

Every day Ignace had asked Omar what he had found, and every day Omar had nothing to say. Now he itched to tell him. Pasteur bent over his microscope.

'Louis? Can I ask you something?'

'Hmm?'

'I don't know how to test it, my idea.'

'Electron microscope. Look at the blood – yours and some from a subject.'

'What? How do you know what I'm thinking?'

'Your doodles on that piece of paper.'

'You were looking?'

'Wouldn't you be looking? Well done: you might be right. You need to see how the protein molecules fold. Shall we get some blood now?'

'Yes!'

Omar was too keen. Something roused inside him at the thought of going to the subjects and taking blood. Pasteur smiled.

'Ah, the keenness of the young scientist,' he said. Pasteur took a pouch of blood from a refrigerated cupboard.

'Shouldn't we use fresh blood?' Omar asked, his stomach tight with anxiety.

'The proteins will be the same. But if you wish.'

Omar followed Pasteur, impatient, trying to hurry him along. But they didn't go to the cages.

They went instead to something like a clinic with everything behind glass. Why had he assumed they'd draw blood themselves from someone?

On the other side of a thick, glass shield someone out of sight filled a syringe from a hairy arm poking through a hole in a metal sheet. The sight of so much blood made Omar feel faint. They wouldn't need it all: how could he get the rest?

The tube of blood came in a heat-sealed plastic bag. Omar, filled with longing, looked at it in Pasteur's hand. At least he couldn't taste it in the air.

Back in the lab, Pasteur cut open the package. Omar made a grab for the tube – he couldn't stop himself – and when Pasteur held it out of his way, Omar lunged at him.

'Woa! What's going on?' shouted Pasteur. But

Omar prised the tube from his hand and fumbled with the lid. He lifted the tube to his lips, his hands trembling with excitement, and poured the blood into his mouth.

He thought he'd pass out. He'd never felt anything so intense. The world seemed to disappear around him, lost in a flood of red that spread warmth to every part of his mind and body. He licked hungrily around the tube, desperate for every drop. And it was gone.

'Take me back there!' he shouted at Pasteur. 'Get more!' He grabbed Pasteur's arm. And then he felt a brief, sharp pain in the back of his neck and a firm hand on his shoulder.

'One, two, three, four ... ' Slow counting of seconds leaked through the red blur in Omar's brain. At ten, the world started to come back into focus. He released Pasteur's arm and started to cry. He cried at the loss of the feeling, and with shame at what he'd done to his friend. Dmitri Ivanovski held him in his thin arms, laying the syringe aside.

'Why have you not been taking ProVamp, manikin? I cannot inject you every time you forget.'

At last, Omar whispered that he had been taking ProVamp, that he didn't understand why he craved blood with such fury, but that Ignace knew – he'd seen it in the hall of cages.

'Ignace knows? And he does nothing?' It was the first time Omar had seen Pasteur angry.

'Then he does it on purpose,' said Ivanovski.

'You've been to the hall of cages?' Pasteur said. 'I have only heard of it. Why did he take you there?'

'To choose a subject.'

Pasteur bristled. 'Why are you so favoured, I wonder?'

'It is not favour,' said Ivanovski. 'It is torment.'

Eight

When Ignace came at noon, Omar ached to tell him his theory, but Pasteur spoke first.

'Omar had an ... episode. With a blood sample. But he says he's taking ProVamp. Can you explain that?'

Ignace waved a hand, as if dismissing the question.

'He hasn't been taking it. He can take it again now. I'll have the pills in his room switched.'

'Switched?' Pasteur raised an eyebrow.

'He's been taking dummy tablets – they contained no ProVamp. Just a little experiment.'

'An experiment?! You *experimented* on him? We need him! What are you thinking? Experimentation is *our* job, not yours!' Pasteur roared.

Ignace held Pasteur's gaze. 'It's not your place to tell me what I may do. I needed Omar to want blood because I had to test that girl on him – Ava, the one from the forest. In Hungary, I fed her vampire blood to make her immune. I needed to know that it had worked. If she was immune, Omar wouldn't want her blood. And he didn't.'

'And what if he *had* wanted her? You would have let him have her? Why him?' Omar sensed Pasteur would have wanted the girl himself. Of course, he thought, Pasteur comes from a time when vampires fed on humans. He must miss it.

'Because he's a new type of vampire, and she ate a new vampire's blood,' Ignace said. 'We have to be certain it's the same.'

'Of course it's the same!' Pasteur said, too loudly. 'He just caught it in a different way.'

'But you don't know that, do you Louis? You've been here more than a hundred years and you still don't know how this disease works.' Omar flinched for Pasteur; Ignace was goading him.

'*He* does – Omar. The one you're experimenting on,' Pasteur said.

Ignace's eyes flashed, the argument forgotten. 'Tell me.'

'Prions,' Omar said. 'Misfolded proteins. Like mad cow disease.'

'Go on,' said Pasteur, watching Omar carefully.

'A prion is a protein that's gone wrong. And it changes other proteins to be the same.'

'Show me how,' Ignace said.

Omar took up a pen and started to draw, but realised he couldn't. Then it struck him. He folded the paper into a bird.

'Origami?' Ignace's voice mocked him.

'Wait,' said Pasteur. 'He's right.'

Omar held up what he'd made: 'A bird.' Then he unfolded it, and refolded it. 'Or a bat?' he said. 'Same paper, differently folded. The same happens to proteins. A normal protein is a bird. The prion is a bat. And the bat goes through the body, refolding all the birds into bats.

'Which protein?' asked Pasteur. 'There are millions.'

'I don't know,' said Omar. 'But I'd guess it's in blood. Maybe haemoglobin.'

'How does it do this?' asked Ignace, spreading his arms wide. 'How does it make me a vampire?'

'It changes things,' said Omar. 'It changes how blood carries oxygen. It must be transmitted in the blood. That's why the mosquito worked. One molecule from a previous victim – just one misfolded protein – will refold all the others. It's in every drop of your blood.'

'You're wrong,' Ignace said. The girl – Ava –

she's immune. We proved that – you didn't want her. In the forest, I made her eat bread soaked in Nathan's blood, remember? It's an old peasant trick to make people immune to us. It's like having injections as a baby. When immune, they don't taste right, they don't attract us.'

'But I can't make that work here,' Pasteur said. 'I can't make people immune.'

'She's not immune,' said Omar. 'She's a vampire.'

Ignace and Omar stared at each other.

'You pricked her, and she didn't bleed,' Omar said.

'Louis – can you be immune to a prion disease?' Ignace demanded.

'I don't know – I've not studied it.'

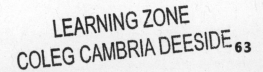

'So she *might* be immune. How do we find out?'

Pasteur mumbled into his beard.

'Speak up, man!'

'We infect someone. From her.'

'No!' shouted Omar. 'It's easy – see if she wants blood. Test her.' Even as he said it, he realised this could give him another chance to see Ava. Perhaps a chance to get her out, and to get out himself. The idea of escape started to seep into the edges of his mind.

'We don't have her,' Ignace said at last. 'She was immune. She's been dumped.'

'Dumped?' Omar's fury made his voice shrill. 'She's not just a bit of waste!'

'Of course not. But she's not useful to us.'

'Did you put a trace on her?' asked Pasteur.

'No, I didn't bother. We can find her – it won't take long.'

'Possibly too long, if she's infected!' Pasteur glowered. 'You were hasty.'

'I wanted her out of here. We drugged her, but you can never tell. Sometimes they remember again.'

'No one would believe her, Ignace,' Pasteur said. 'But you need to find her. You've just released a vampire who doesn't even know she's a vampire.'

'How could she not know? *We* changed overnight,' said Omar. 'It's been weeks.'

Pasteur shrugged. 'Different method. Ingestion might take effect more slowly. We can't tell. In the old days, vampires could bite the same person for months without them changing. They probably weren't infected. Usually, they're infected at some point and 'die' – like you did in the forest. Often they're buried, but then they come back.'

'How do they get out of the grave? All that earth on top of them?' asked Omar.

'Grave-diggers are not well paid.' Pasteur rubbed his thumb and finger together, showing they were paid bribes.

'Find her,' he said sternly to Ignace.

'Don't tell me what to do!' Ignace snapped.

'You shouldn't have released her without proper testing,' Pasteur said. 'If you don't find her, and she's turned, we have trouble. Big trouble.'

Nine

Omar woke early to another snowy day. Large flakes whirled outside his window. How long had he been in Yakutsk? Perhaps ten days, two weeks? He'd had enough. He thought suddenly of his aunt, who believed he was in New York. She'd looked after him for ten years, since he arrived in the UK, and she'd be worried. His phone didn't work – the castle walls, a metre thick, must be blocking the signal. He had to get out. If Ava had gone, there was no need to wait longer.

He wasn't due in the lab for another hour. He dressed in all his clothes to be as warm as possible. Then he crept through the corridors, following the outside walls. At last, he found a door so low it was probably a rubbish chute or coal hatch. Locked, of course, but it had a keypad. He prayed the code was the same for every door: 20041889. Something clicked inside the mechanism – yes!

He didn't push the door open imediately. He remembered the first locked door, Ignace's Bluebeard room. Who was in there? He didn't think he could get them out, but he hated to leave someone locked away – they'd probably done nothing.

He ran through the corridors, making a mental note of every turn so that he didn't get lost, and came back to the locked grille. No one was around. He didn't touch anything – another alert from Ignace's paramilitaries would be disastrous.

'Hello?' he called in a loud whisper. 'Anyone there?'

Shuffling, clanking chains, but no voice answered.

'I don't know if you speak English,' Omar went on. 'But the number to get out is 2-0-0-4-1-8-8-9. Remember it. 2004 1889. Good luck.'

And he ran back through the corridors.

Omar pushed against the door he had unlocked. Snow piled up outside made it hard to shift. But then a blast of cold air savaged his face.

Now he was outside, he knew he wouldn't go back. He wasn't just going to call his aunt – he was going to run.

There were twenty metres of open ground before the trees. And then, he knew, the razor wire. He pulled his hands inside his sleeves and sprinted across the clearing. Just within the tree line was a small shed with its door ajar. He wondered if it contained anything useful.

Inside, body bags lay piled on the floor.

Horrified, Omar ran blindly on. When he paused for breath, leaning against a tree, he heard a tiny sound – the creaking of metal. Something was moving in the wind. He realised that the sound came from above. Omar looked up.

Over his head, a man hung from a branch. He wore a green jumpsuit, like the one Omar had arrived in. His bare feet were chained together and the chain creaked as he moved in the wind. Omar gasped and felt bile rise in his throat. He ran again, this time towards the razor wire fence.

He planned to follow it to a gate, but in a couple of minutes he came to a wide pool. He bent forward, clutching at the stitch in his side, and wondered if he dare cross the ice.

Before he had time to decide, he heard barking. A flash of white and grey dashed to and fro between the trees, and then headed straight for him. A large dog, a husky perhaps, loped easily over the snow. Omar looked ahead at the ice – would it bear his weight? Then he glanced back at the dog, approaching fast. A figure in a long grey coat and a fur hat appeared through the trees. The man raised a rifle and took aim at Omar.

Ten

'OK,' Omar shouted, 'OK, I've stopped. Look, I've got my hands up! Don't shoot!'

The man lowered the rifle and spoke into a phone as he walked towards Omar. Omar stood shivering with fright and cold, his hands over his head. In a moment the dog had reached him. It bared its teeth and snarled, and Omar shrank backwards. The man said something in Russian and the dog stood still, guarding Omar.

A moment later, a second man hurried through the trees. It was Ignace. Omar wasn't sure whether he was more afraid of the dog or the vampire.

'What are you doing out here, Omar?'

Although his voice was stern, Ignace didn't shout at him.

'I – I need to get in touch with my aunt,' he said at last. 'She'll be worried about me. There's no signal inside.'

'I'm not inclined to believe you.'

'Can I phone her?' Omar pleaded.

'No, you can't. There's no signal inside or outside. And the place is not on maps – nor Google Earth. So even if there was a signal, no one would come for you.'

'How?' Omar asked, suddenly more isolated and frightened than ever.

'The pine forests never change, summer or winter. The roof's painted to look like forest. You're nowhere – a hundred kilometres from the nearest town. You can't walk a hundred kilometres in minus 20 degrees without a coat, Omar.'

'That man ... ' Omar began.

'Which man?' Ignace snapped.

'In the tree. Hanging. Is he alive?'

'How serious are you about science, Omar?' Ignace sounded weary. 'No, he is not alive. You've stumbled into our body farm.'

'Did you kill him?'

Ignace didn't answer, but stooped to clear snow from the ice of the pool with his gloved hand.

'Look – here's another of our experiments.'

Omar looked down through the ice into the white face of a girl with blue eyes. He staggered backwards. Bubbles under the ice made it look as if she blinked.

'You're a monster!' he screamed. 'What is this place? You said it was a research lab – but what you do here is inhuman!'

'Calm down, Omar.'

'Were they dead when they got here?' Omar tried again, struggling to keep control of his horror.

'Some were. Some were not. There are sometimes ... accidents. As there are with any large research project.'

'Are they vampires?' Omar asked.

Ignace shrugged. 'Some are. It's all part of Pasteur's virus work. And now it will be useful for your prion work, don't you think? You've done well. Do you wish to see more?'

Omar shook his head.

'I didn't kill them for these experiments, Omar,' Ignace said. 'Some are brought in dead. Some are not as dead as they look.'

Omar stared down at the girl under the ice and wondered whether she had blinked. Could a vampire do that? Lie under the ice without dying? He wanted to ask, but didn't want to engage with Ignace's experiments.

'You wouldn't want to try to escape, Omar. It's a hostile landscape, as you can see. You'll go home when you've finished. When *I've* finished with *you*. It will not be so long.'

'Why me?' Omar asked, his voice rising in spite of himself. 'I don't know enough, I'm not even a student yet.'

'No, you're not. You'll go home, go to Oxford, learn all you can — all you need — and you'll come back later. We have all the time in the world.'

Omar didn't want to come back. Ignace raised a hand to silence him before he could say so.

'What you want is of no interest to me,' Ignace went on. 'The greater good is more important than that. You have a duty to serve your fellows.'

'I didn't ask to become a vampire,' Omar snapped. 'I don't want any of this. I don't want to be in your creepy castle, I don't want to experiment on people – and I don't want to come back. Ever.'

Ignace smiled.

'No. And you don't want to prey on the drop-outs on the London underground, do you? Or feast on animals you can catch in the slums – rats, foxes, pigeons? It's this research centre that has freed us from living like that, Omar. *We* made ProVamp. Don't imagine that the great drug companies care about us. We have to find out about our condition, develop our own medicines. We have to look after our own – and you're one of us now.

'Come, let's go inside. You can go home soon and continue this work later. Much later. You have hundreds of years to get used to it, Omar.'

'Where's Ava?' Omar asked, suddenly afraid that she, too, was an experiment.

'She's somewhere in Kosovo. We need to find her.'

'Can I help? To find her?' Omar asked.

Ignace raised an eyebrow.

'So you *are* interested in her?'

Omar cursed his clumsiness.

'Not like that. I – I just ... '

'Well, it seems perhaps she is a vampire after all. Perhaps you can help find her. And then – who knows?

But first you must finish your work.'

Vampire Dawn

The story starts with **Die Now or Live Forever**. Read it first.

Then follow each individual's story. You can read these in any order:

Juliette's story

Finn's story

Omar's story

Alistair and Ruby's story

Ava's story

Plus an essential guide for new vampires.